PREETVIK- A tale of two crazy souls

SOUMYA RANJAN

ISBN 978-93-5610-063-3

Published in India 2022 by Pencil

Contributors:
Editor: Smriti Sudha and Soumya"s Team

A brand of
One Point Six Technologies Pvt. Ltd.
123, Building J2, Shram Seva Premises,
Wadala Truck Terminal, Wadala (E)
Mumbai 400037, Maharashtra, INDIA
E connect@thepencilapp.com
W www.thepencilapp.com

DISCLAIMER: *This is a work of fiction. Names, characters, places, events and incidents are the products of the author's imagination. The opinions expressed in this book do not seek to reflect the views of the Publisher.*

Author biography

Soumya Ranjan has been writing since 2019 when he was just 11. He is known for writing books at a very young age. He published his first book in the year 2020. 'The vital truth', 'Readers pleasure' and 'The National best sellers of India' are some of the books authored by Soumya which are the Indian bestsellers. He is reading in class 9. Love stories and many other stories just flow in his veins. Soumya has been awarded multiple awards for outstanding skills and talent. He writes his book in a very simple language that makes it easy to read and understand.

He got published in the daily newspapers in 2021 when he got recognized in the country. He has been giving numerous interviews on many channels. He loves to make albums, films, and documentaries and some of his videos crossed 200 views in an hour. He also has a keen interest in writing poems and published his first poetry collection in 2021 by notion press which is named 'The vital truth'.

He loves to write stories for children and young adults. He mimics the Bollywood celebrities and his YouTube videos are recommended as funny. He belongs from the city of Jamshedpur and is pursuing in Vidya Bharati Chinmaya Vidyalaya. His teachers and friends praised him and supported him based on his talent. He is one of the youngest stars in his city and is loved by his well-wishers all across the country. This is his second romance novel and it took almost one year to complete this book. He started photography venture @_photo_factree_. He is also a blogger and his blogs are also loved by some celebrities.

He is also crazy about dancing in beats and he is also known for his humorous nature. He is a designer and his content is loved all over the country.

Connect him via:

Email: joinauthorsoumya@gmail.com

Instagram : its__real__soumyaranjan

Twitter: @its_soumya

Youtube: Soumya Ranjan author.

CONTENTS

PRAISES 14

LOVE BEGINS 17

WHEN I MET HER 19

SHWETA PROPOSED ME 29

THE SCHOOL TRIP AND FIGHT WITH PREETI ... 38

WE WERE IN A RELATIONSHIP 50

COLLEGE LIFE 66

PREETI COMMITTED SUICIDE 78

A HAPPY ENDING 95

Glossary 108

List of Contributors 115

Preface

In life, we often think that it shouldn't end like this. We expect the sun to shine bright, flowers to bloom, but sometimes the day turns dark and leaves us disappointed. Not because there's no daylight, but because we all want a perfect ending. We forget that in real life, the reality is mostly far different from our imagination. Here, verses of life don't always rhyme, and beats of the heart move quicker than the beats of life. Life doesn't begin with a 'happy' new year, nor does it end with the same spirit. What's more, it doesn't even stop when you lose someone you couldn't once live without. Life simply doesn't begin or end. Life goes on. You still breathe, you still care, and you still live.

I somehow have my calling - being a writer, a humorous person, sweet, caring, or a designer. I always listen to my heart whenever I start writing a book. People see the success but the hardship they don't. I faced rejections several times and I told myself that writing is shit and I can never pursue it.

But God is always fair and I wonder in 2020 when no one guided me, no one supported me and no one even read my stories but my first book made everyone delighted. All I need is to be appreciated and loved and luckily I am because art can never go unnoticed and I live for it. My first book was just among my friends and relatives but how my book got popular among the readers was just unpredictable.

My heart got recognized, no matter how many people loved it and how many hated it. Making documentaries and writing are far apart and I have experience with both but still, I have a lot to experience.

In an interview, I have been asked a question who is my inspiration and my answer is always the same.' In the universe each organism, it can be living or non-living too, have something in them that makes me inspired.'

People think that writing is a waste of paper, time, and energy but nobody can replace writing as no story - no film.

You may fail million times before you kiss success and that's what I learned from my journey of 4 years. Mistakes, failure, insult, somebody being jealous of you, frustration and rejection are part of your progress and growth in your life. Nobody ever achieved anything, worthwhile without facing these things.

Into my personal not, I am not rich or a very wealthy person but when I see a person facing hunger, then my wallet gets empty. And this is what I wanted every people to do if it's possible for them. I may not be handsome but I can give my hand to some. The start of my NGO is not only to help but to get happy feelings and blessings from all across the world and I hope you do the same.

You get a chance to face your life once and it's your choice to make it good or bad.

Till now, I wrote a lot of things that motivated you and now let me share something very interesting...

When I was a child, I visited Kolkata for spending my vacation. I was holding my mother's hand and accidentally in a crowd, I picked another woman's hand. After a couple of minutes of walking, I saw that I was with another woman and her son is with my mom.

I was confused and looked at her face and we both were puzzled. A big confusion was created and I called my mom loudly and we burst out laughing.

The reason behind telling the story is that we are being so busy with our online and offline life that we even forget about those who loved and cared for us. I hope that you spend time with your family, friends also with your relationships.

Spread love and get loved. I hope that you all are safe and happy and thank you for picking up this book for reading.

-Love from your dearest

Soumya.

Acknowledgements

Congratulations – you picked a book! You left Youtube, Instagram, Whatsapp, and whatever exciting stuff and picked up my book.

I would like to express my gratitude to a lot of people who saw me growing with this. It's always difficult to write an acknowledgment. A lot has changed in the past few years, but I am glad that there are certain relationships and people who haven't changed even a bit.

I will begin by thanking my parents for their unconditional love and blessing. Though my mom is facing some bad obstacles still her love is beyond expectations.

I would like to thank my sister for her faith and encouragement. My friends Hardik, Preet, Aditi, Saurabh, Madhu, Antima, Sadaf, Ishaan, and many more for consistently believing in me and helping me in every possible thing.

I would like to thank my teacher, especially Poonam Mam, Manjula mam, Mina mam, Man Singh Sir, Vipin Mam, Surupa Mam, Meera mam, Tania Mam, Veenita Mam, Rakhi mam, Niharika mam, Payal mam, and Abhijeet Sir who consistently motivated me and for being with me through every phase of my life and guiding me on what's right and wrong both personally and professionally.

I am amazingly fortunate to have some lovely seniors like Dixita didi, Priya Didi, Prerna Didi, and Varun bhaiya who make my life better and more interesting. I like to thank my grandfather for believing in me.

I am grateful to Mr. Ajitabha, one of the most humble people, Devanshi mam, Rohit Dawesar sir, Himanshu sir, and the whole Soumya Ranjan team for their outstanding work, all of you are inarguably brilliant.

I would thank my publisher for the extraordinary kindness and after the performance of my previous book 'The National bestsellers of India '.

A big thank you to Rohit Sir and Priya mam for allowing me to add them in the cover page.

Also, I would like to thank the delivery agents for handover my book to the readers.

The covid pandemic raging this year meant I couldn't travel enough but I love my cousins who stay a bit far and their support is too captivating.

Thanks to all my readers for making my day. I love all those comments, e-mails, and messages that you send me on daily basis and I try my best to reply to each one of you.

Thanks for making me work hard. You guys have a big hand in making me what I am today. A big hug to all of you and Life wouldn't have been the same without you all.

If I missed anyone I am really sorry and please forgive me for any of my mistakes.

Love from your dearest

Soumya

Introduction

Soumya comes up with his new book which deals with true love, friendship, and full of dreams. This book is a really full package of humour, horror, and emotions. India's youngest writer, Soumya Ranjan shares the unique love story of Souvik and Preeti.

What is true love? Is it that 'mele babu ne khana khaya'?

No, true love is a strong and lasting affection. Souvik's and Preeti'sī5 love story is beyond emotion. It connected two hearts, two bodies together in a positive mode. Both the love birds are from Jamshedpur. Preeti wanted to pursue banking and Preeti's dream was to become an actor but his family didn't support him. Preeti met an accident but true love never sets apart but Preeti's decision of committing suicide made a drastic change in their story.

What lies ahead? She died or was alive? Was there love set incomplete?

Where will destiny lead them?

This is another heart-warming tale of love, friendship, and dreams.

PRAISES

Praises

"You really write fantastic and I hope you will reach great heights."

-Raghubar das (Former Chief Minister of Jharkhand and vice president of BJP)

I adore you for the extraordinary work you are doing at this small age

-Puppindar Singh(Ollywood actor)

You are doing a fabulous job Saumya and may God bless you

-Arshi Bharti (actor of TMKOC)

Happy to see you rising and making Jamshedpur feel proud

-Saryu Roy (Member of legislative assembly, Jamshedpur and Minister of Water Department)

I am proud of you Soumya and I hope you will do one's upmost

-Delnaaz Irani (Bollywood actor)

"Good to see you doing such a noble work of starting an NGO and writing books at such a small age"

-Ruskin bond (Indian writer)

"One day will surely meet you and I am also happy to talk to you and your work is just unbelievable."

-Arjun Munda (Minister of Tribal Affairs of India)

"You are too talented Soumya, both in academics and aesthetics"

- Vipin Sharma (National Awardee)

" Jamshedpur is feeling prominent to have you in our city"

- Prabhat Khabar

" Soumya's believe in love has inspired the youth and the young generation"

-Dainik Jagran

"Unbelievable work Soumya and I wish you all the best for your future endeavors "

-Sapna Thakur (TV serial actor)

"Thank you so much, Soumya for writing such love stories and interesting stories"

-The telegraph.

LOVE BEGINS

It is not your conversation
That keeps me entertained
But rather the way you look at me
That makes me feel sustained
It's the curve of your lips
And the curl of your hair
It's all of the little things
That makes me stop and stare

It is not your intelligence
That drew me close to you
It is not your sense of humor
That has thrown me all askew
It's the touch of your hand
And the thoughts in your head
It's all of the little things
The things that don't get said

It's not your vivid history
That's made me fall in love
It's not your comprehension
Of the world or what's above
It is your soft temperament
And the way you smile at me
It's all of the little things

That makes me want to see

It's not when we are talking
That I want to know some more
It is not whilst you teach me
I learn what I'm looking for
It is the time we spend alone
And the time in utter silence
It's all of the little things
That form a strong alliance

It's not the job you work so hard
That shows your true commitment
It's not your crazy habits
That gives me great fulfillment
It is the way you use your hands
And the way I have been chosen
It's all of the little things
Why I know silence is golden

WHEN I MET HER

In winter days, getting up early for school was a big refrain for me. My father used to shout if I get up late. I don't want that my father should acclaim throat pain as he keeps on shouting the whole day and night.

So, I usually get up early to make my room clean. I feel like, the blankets are yelling at me, to keep them also tidy in the bed corner. I was in a sleepy mood and fell from the bed. My father being an Indian parent started hitting me instead of asking that have I got hurt or not...

He started bawling "Can't you see I am weeping the floor and you bastard fell on the wet floor and all the water got split. Go fast and get a bath immediately." My eyes were still swirling and I went to the hall and slept on the sofa. My sleep cycle was a big progeny for me.

My father with the broomstick gave a very painful gesture on my ass. I shouted "Ouch! Who's that" in a rude voice and then I suddenly saw he was none other than my father, and as a usual one more painful gesture. My bums were reddened like a tomato. Slowly and steadily I went to the brush holder. I picked up my brush and applied toothpaste to it. I didn't like to use Patanjali toothpaste but there was no one to listen to mine. I was brushing so fast, that it took almost 20 minutes to complete my brushing. Now, the most difficult level was to take a bath and that too in winters. I went to the kitchen searched for the hot water and poured it into the bucket. However, I took a bath and washed my dirty clothes with India's most trusted washing powder Ghadi- Pehle istemal kare fir Vishwas kare. My clothes were the same when I used to wash with any other washing powder but the advertising agents just tattle like anything

Dressed up into fine, ironed clothes made me look smarter and more handsome. I am fond of doing a lot of experiments on my face. I used to apply a lot of creams and glow powders before going to school. My sister was like a Hitler and she used to interrupt in all my matters and well it was her bachpan ka adhikar to complain papa. So I often call her "papa ki pari". She enquired in a serious and dumpy mood "Why do you apply such remedies on your face, before going to school? Neither you are going to attend a marriage function nor are you going to choose a girl for you." While applying the talcum powder, I threw some on her face and ran away. She shouted "You moron." I was just against those who used harsh words. I went nearer to her and gave a punch and pushed her as I didn't like anyone being from a good family, using such kind of words. I warned her telling that if she repeats those words, then I would complain to mother. She stared at me for 5 seconds and again used the same words. She told "Go, and say to mom...... mummy ka chamcha saala." She was sometimes too annoying and my habit was to ignore her. It was time for school and my mother packed my school tiffin. She was sympathetic, opulent, and a splendour lady. She was a teacher in a private school and I loved being taught by her. The morning was too refreshing and the sun had just arrived to say goodbye to school. Monday mornings were usually considered lazy and a bit of harassment but I speculate Monday mornings as the most interesting day because, after a gap of two days, we would be greeting our friends and teachers. Since childhood, I was a very naughty guy, always restless in the classroom. My teachers had a long list waiting to be put in front of my parents. My father always worried about me and what will I do when I grow up. I was 90 percent passionate about my studies and managed to score almost perfect. My friends came from various categories. Some were toppers, some were like me and some were hopeless in the sense of both: discipline and academics.

My bag was filled with books and excitement. Just there were few minutes left to arrive at school and Yes! I was at the campus. We did chit-chatting in the assembly. Many students assembled as Monday was the day when our school principal used to address the children and handle the assembly. I used to adore my principal a lot. Her personality and the royal walk made her more attractive. Before the assembly started, we assembled in a queue. I never like talking a lot but if they are girls, then I can talk for the whole day. That day was the shuffling day of my class and my friends would get separated from me and when I got to know about the scuffle, that was the saddest moment for me. My class teacher called out the names one by one and they were the ones who left our class and shifted to another section. Some students came to our class but I spotted one girl who belonged to section A, who was so radiant and attractive that my heartbeat raised to 172 times in a minute. I just shifted my place and sat one bench behind her. My class teacher was taking the attendance but I was still daydreaming for her. She threw chalk on me which hit directly on my forehead. I was distracted from her and was scolded too. That girl who came from section A, knew me, but we were not so friendly but I wanted to be a good friend of hers. I was curious to know her name and when my teacher was taking the attendance, I got to know her name and it was Preeti. She described the natural beauty. She described simplicity and her aura made my surroundings brighter than ever. When she blinked her eyes, her eyelashes touched my heart. I was just dying to talk to her but my Kamine friends would just start spreading rumors. Her deep black eyes, sweet smile, and shiny black hair made me fly high in the sky with the angels. It was the third period of our class and the students were excited to attend that class as it was our P.T period.

We all gathered outside and assembled ourselves in a queue. She was standing in the third number of the queue and I too stood in the third number of the boy's queue believing that whichever girl stood opposite to the boy, they get married in future. Yes, it was a stupid thought. We all strived towards the ground and of course, the boys started playing their preferred games. Some were playing kho-kho, kabaddi and many more but that day I was a bit apart from the team. I was just roaming in the ground as my eyes were not ready to leave Preeti. She had an allurement personality which made my darling heart bump again and again. Preeti's hair was brown with blond highlights. She neatly used to part it from the centre and applied just a clip to hold the strands. She sometimes did plates in her hair. She applied no makeup and was completely against it. I went nearer to her but didn't have the valour to talk to her. She was roaming with her friends and slipped on the mud. I thought of holding her and wanted to create a romantic scene which we used to see in movies and serials but it was the school ground and holding her was an exceptional incident. I was feeling very hurt and deviated from not helping her. She didn't hurt herself much but fell very badly and her friends helped her out. I went towards her and offered some water and it was so captivating to see, that she held my bottle and drank the water. It was the happiest moment for me on that day.

I used to pretend that I am paying attention to what the teacher is teaching but I used to spend the time daydreaming as Preeti's beauty casted a spell over me.

Remembering those days was like a gem to me. Days passed by, slowly and steadily we became good friends. Making her a good friend of mine was the first plan which was successfully executed. I not only loved her from the bottom of my heart but from top to end of my darling heart. She was like a sweet addiction for me but as we know before starting up with good work, some of the other ones will come to interfere in your life and of course, that person came. Shobhit was the one, who was hated by the entire school and I too hated him because he was obstructing my love life. He too had a crush on Preeti and it was with a bad intention. Preeti hated him the most as he was the one who neither respected girls nor the teachers. Preeti was a girl who always took discipline as her first priority. Every teacher hated Shobhit due to his dirty behavior. There was not only one obstruction in my life, the other creature was Shweta who had a crush on me.

When I acknowledged this, I was amazed, for what? I too didn't know.

Shweta was a Bengali fat girl, who just wanted my fellowship. I was in fear that if she proposes to me, then what will I answer?

I skipped thinking about Shweta and jumped towards Preeti.

While arts period was going on, Preeti sat behind me and she just swiped her paintbrush towards me for just fun, but my moron friends took this in a bad way. Preeti painted a beautiful painting and was praised by our drawing teacher.

I was left with the blank sheet. My drawing teacher glared at my paper and told me to stand up.

"Why haven't you started drawing?" The teacher asked

"Sir……" I was left with nothing to utter in front of him.

"Just shut up! Don't make any excuses…." He angrily burst on me and pulled my ears.

I kept quiet and saw Preeti whispering something to Shweta in her ears.

"It should be completed within a week" My drawing teacher warned.

I nodded with innocence on my face. I kept staring at Preeti, but her innocent face melts my anger.

Besides me, there was a girl Aditi, whom I usually shared my thoughts and I felt that she must be understanding better than my crush Preeti. Aditi was a smart, talented, and extraordinary girl. Her personality was at a good effect, especially on Shobhit. Shobhit was a stupid fellow as I told you earlier and he used every girl as a timepass.

Aditi never fell for him but rumours decided that she was in love. Ha! Ha! Ha! .....

Aditi was talented too but in some other field. The tap-tap sound came into my ears and we saw our history teacher entering our class to start her boring lecture and she announced about our final exams which will be held in February.

"Now stop this commotion and concentrate on your respective books," She yelled.

There was pin-drop silence in her class and she started teaching. I was just waiting for the bell to ring. My ears were tormented to hear the bell ring. Finally, the bell rang and we were ready to get dispersed. Now, the time came for our final examination and I started studying day and night to score well because I was somewhat a studious guy. We were in the examination hall waiting for the question paper and my heart was doing 'dhak-dhak' rapidly.

It was maths test, and all questions were somehow manageable to answer. It took me almost I hour 30 minutes to complete the paper.

The more half-an-hour was left for the bell to ring but I took some advantage of time and gazed at Preeti. The time was over and we all submitted our paper. While I was heading towards downstairs, a sweet voice called "Souvik".

I turned and saw that it was Preeti who called me. She forwarded her hands to me and said "can we be good friends?" I was like a cloud in nine and too forwarded my hands for friendship. I remember those days and feel like laughing loudly.

I thought that she was also falling for me but her friend Shweta always poked her nose in my love life. She too forwarded her hands and repeated the same line "Can we be good friends?" I just shook my hands with a drowsy face but she still gave a smile and went downstairs. Preeti belonged to a very decent family and she had a sister who was elder than her. I was just not able to concentrate on any of my tasks as I was in love for the first time. It was all going like a film. I started thinking about Preeti's future and mine too.

23rd March 2019: It is the day when everyone prays to god but I had faith in my determination. Walking into the class with my parents for the report card was a danger zone for me. I saw Preeti sitting there with her father and I felt like touching his feet as he would be my future father-in-law. My tensed face was vanished by seeing Preeti. My class teacher called Preeti's name and she was happy to announce that she bagged the first position in the class. I was so ecstatic by seeing her happy face. My father whispered, "Learn something from Preeti."

After Preeti's turn, my class teacher called my name and gave me the report card, and I bagged the fourth position in my class. My class teacher gave some virtuous remarks. My father was fortunate to see the result and left the class. While coming downstairs, he was just giving his boring lectures on life and career. "I am happy seeing your result but you should work harder. You should make me proud and I don't know what will take place in your future days and that's the reason I shout on you to work hard." His lectures were going on till I reached my home. My family was eagerly waiting to judge me on the basis on my result. My mother was happy to see the result. I dressed up myself in my home clothes and started playing badminton with my friend.

This was a true Joy which I miss nowadays. I was very passionate about archery and the reason behind learning archery more passionately was Preeti as she also learned archery with me.

Teacher's Day

We were celebrating Teachers Day and we wanted to make the day memorable. Well, I was decorating the board, I saw Aditi with Shobhit. They were laughing and I wanted her to be on the right path as it was my duty, as a good friend.

I stopped Aditi and advised her to stay apart from him and then I was busy with my board decoration. Shweta came nearer to me and started helping me. She was totally mad at me and now she wanted my company. Our teacher entered our class, we didn't let her teach a single thing.

We were just in a mood to chill and have fun. I saw Preeti with blond highlights as she had a fair complexion, her smile made her look cute.

Describing her gave me another level of happiness...

We were all in a Jolly mood but Preeti was looking a bit gloomy that day. I went to her and greeted "Hii Preeti ".

"Hello" in a low tone she replied

"Why is your face looking downhearted today?"

"It's because none of my friends bought gifts for me as it is my birthday today and nobody has wished me too."

I was smiling from within because I knew about her birthday and I had also planned a surprise for her.

"Ok, don't worry, it might have got skipped from their mind"

After the day was over Preeti's friends and I took her to the Auditorium to give her a surprise. Her eyes were filled with tears and she was also thankful to us. I was very glad to see her happy face. After cake cutting ceremony Poonam (Preeti's friend) declared "It's all because of Souvik, he planned the entire party, or else your birthday would have been colourless". She saw me with a very lovely sight.

"Thank you so much for making my day so special" Preeti thanked me in a sweet and soothing voice.

SHWETA PROPOSED ME

Getting up early for school gave me immense pleasure. I used to pack up my bag in the morning and I was unable to find my Sanskrit book.

Searching for my Sanskrit book wasted 15 minutes of my day but I was still incapable to find my book.

At last, I fetched it from my sister's bag... well she was not at home, or else she would have got a harsh treatment from me.

I was dressed up and was looking handsome. I hung up my bag and was off to school.

When I arrived at school it seemed as Shweta was waiting for me, since morning.

She just came near to me and started singing romantic songs of "Dilwale Dulhaniya Le Jayenge".

I ignored her and ran to the assembly in search of Preeti.

Shweta had already informed some of her friends that she had a crush on me and would propose to me.

I was unknown to the fact that she would propose to me.

Shweta was waiting for the right moment to propose to me and I was waiting for the right moment to reject her.

She started acting very weird, made me feel cramped, meanwhile, our principal arrived at the assembly to address us and I loved hearing her speak.

She was a very acumen teacher and hearing her talk encouraged and inspired me.

Now the Assembly was on the way to get over and we were heading towards our class and meanwhile, Shweta was trying to interact with me. I had no engross talking to her but she was very irritating.

I just felt like breaking the line and reaching the class but my bad luck. As I entered the class, at the same moment I was out of the class too.

"Ma'am what I do?"

"Yes, u did nothing. Neither you did ur homework nor did you buy your copy"

"But Ma'am I did the homework but forgot to bring the copy"

“Shut up and don't argue! Don’t give me such silly excuses" she growled on me like she would chew me the sudden moment.

I moved out of the class Shweta at her place and told "excuse me Ma'am! I too didn't do my homework and not bought the copy too".

“That’s a very proud feeling Shweta, isn't it?

Are you waiting for me to throw you out of the class?" She taunted Shweta.

She was not at all ashamed to be out of the class as she just wanted to spend leisure time with me. "I too forgot to bring my copy "she started the conversation. I with no reply.

"Are you upset on any issue?"

"Say something” She added.

“Please! Stop that." I replied in a rude steady voice.

She was numbed, I went inside and told my teacher "Sorry mam for the mistake” and as expected, she made me sit inside her class. Then I told Preeti to check Shweta's bag...

Preeti got Shweta's mathematics notebook in her bag and as I expected she lied to the teacher.

Preeti told Mrs. Manju (maths teacher) about Shweta's math notebook. Mrs. Manju called Shweta inside the class.

She just raised the copy and asked "what is this?"

"Sorry mam I think I have not checked my back properly"

"Don't try to act smart Shweta" banging the copy on the desk MS Manju yelled.

It was a busy day as every teacher handed in some of the other work.

While I was out of the classroom Shweta changed her place and sat just behind me.

Her intent was to come closer to me and also she expected to be my girlfriend.

She was just like a 'chipku gum' and she was not at all ready to leave me.

She intentionally started touching me and I was feeling awkward.

The moment I turned back to scold her, she immediately apologizes.

I was getting distracted by Preeti.

Preeti was such an innocent girl but every girl had a kind of jealousy towards Preeti.

One fact I hated in Preeti was that she sometimes inculcated a bad attitude in herself but still I loved and supported her.

As the day was coming to an end, her weird acts were going on increasing.

She was continuously throwing chalk pieces and paper balls at me. After some time my social science teacher entered and requested Shweta to distribute the history notebook among the students, it was like "Sone Pe Suhaga" for Shweta.

My notebook was also added to the pile and she would get a chance to come closer to me...

When the time came for my notebook, she came towards me and gave a smile, and handed over the notebook to me and it seemed like she was in a romantic mood. For what? I was unknown. Sometimes it's very difficult to understand girls and their feelings. If they are happy at some moment, the sudden moment they will be angry too, like Preeti.

I have been experiencing with so many girls like Preeti, Shweta, Aditi, Poonam, and many more. Shweta was always in the mood to start bitching about other girls. This stupid act of doing chugli is a talent of every girl, even the aunties. I love to be a part of the girl's group but I stepped back as I didn't want to be a part of the rumors also.

I was watching the clock and was waiting for the period to end. It was the last period of the day. Just the teacher was on the way to start a new chapter and the bell rang and the happiness for me was unpredictable

Shweta came to me as I was sitting with my friend Anubhav in the school gallery and she started acting like nonsense. She was on the way to propose to me and suddenly when I turned back to drink water I saw her friends were hiding behind the tree and were watching the drama.

Shweta sat near me and that was out of patience level but still, I was quiet. She was trying to be sexy and her being exotic was too much irritating for me. Her acts were very weird like opening her hairband, trying to be hot, and coming closer to me.

"Enough Shweta! What are you trying to do in the school quad?"

"Cool down Souvik, cool down yaar!".

My nostrils were fully reddened but I was still controlling. I was in fear that, if any of my family members catches me with Shweta then I would be hanged up. I was leaving from there and she pulled me back to propose to me.

"Souvik, I love you, I love you from the day I saw you. I am not just in love because you are handsome. I love you because you are kind-hearted, cool, funny, and humble person. I really love you from the bottom of my heart. I was just waiting for the right time to propose you. May you understand my feelings?"

Anubhav was having a crush on Shweta and when he heard that she is proposing me, he was somewhat fainting.

"What" Anubhav surprisingly acted

"Yes Anubhav, I love Souvik the most. "She replied. I saw her friends were enjoying the scene.

I was too astonished by hearing Shweta and what to reply was out of my mind.

She gave me one day time to think and then reply.

The whole day I was just thinking about the incident and there was no one with whom I was able to share my feelings.

The day was spent in confusion and depression and I never ever wanted to break her heart or hurt her but I also didn't want to be in a relationship with her.

The next day Preeti got to know about the incident and her face was expressing that she was feeling jealous but at the same moment her smile washed off the jealousy. I was sitting on my bench and was thinking about the matter. Shweta's friend came to me and asked "Souvik, Have you thought of anything?"

I was not able to hear them as I was daydreaming. Suddenly Poonam clapped and my attention was on them. I replied in a confusing voice "Ye...yes. Yes".

"We are asking that, have you thought of anything? What is your response?"

"Please leave me alone for some time...I am still not ready with the reply "

Shweta with a dazzling smile entered the class. She was just looking at me, she came near to me and my heartbeat was rising, my legs were shaking and my lips were shivering.

"Have you come up with any reply, Souvik?

I was looking at Preeti and her ignorance.

"Na..No.....no" again in a shivering voice I replied...

"How much time do you want?"

The moment I was going to deny her, my class teacher entered.

"Good Morning Ma'am" We greeted

"Good morning students and May I know why is there so much commotion in the class?"

Preeti stood up and I was scared and many questions came into my mind.

"Is she going to tell about yesterday's incident?" I thought but what I heard made me relax.

She told, "Ma'am, today there is a postcard camping and we are going to write a letter to the Prime Minister".

"Oo...Oh! That's great. All the best my dear students."

"Thank you ma'am" we thanked the teacher but Shweta was still gazing at me.

There was a break or usually, we say recess time, and Shweta came to me and again asked the same question "Souvik please reply"

"Shweta, I am sorry but I don't love you because there is someone who is more important than you". I replied and was about to leave.

As I expected, she was hurt and with a smile, she replied "The girl whom you love is the luckiest one, I wish you all the best." She told me in an emotional tone and went back to the seat and was still snorting. I was also feeling pity for her and my intention was not to break her heart. After the dismissal when I was passing through one of the classes, I saw Shweta standing alone near the school park which was behind the school building. I ran towards her and saw that she was about to cut her nerves just because I rejected her.

I ran towards her and slapped her.

"Are you really insane?"

"Don't stop me! Let me do that"

"Listen Shweta, so I can't be your boyfriend but I will remain a very good friend of yours. I will never step back in helping you. Don't even try to take any such step which will hurt your family and friends too. If I rejected you that means I am not that type of boy whom you wanted and I wish that you will get the best life partner." I motivated her, threw the blade, and left.

THE SCHOOL TRIP AND FIGHT WITH PREETI

We were in class 9 and in our school, from class 9 onwards we were sent to excretion (school trip). When the announcement was made by the class teacher about the school trip I was on the ninth cloud and wished to hug my class teacher tightly but it was too close to impossibility.

She wrote a notice on the board and directed us to effigy the same in the diary.

"Dear Parents

Our school has planned for a school trip to Odisha for 1 week. It's very elegant to announce that your child will learn a lot from the sculptures and monuments.

There are certain processes to be done before sending your child:-

1. Do give a consent form with your signature and also attach the child's Aadhar card.

2. You have to do a payment of rupees 1500(online payment is also accepted), the link for the payment is on our school website.

3. The Last date for submission is 15 December 2022."

After copying down the notice, everyone started a conversation with their friends. I saw Preeti was unhappy and the reason was that the fees were too much.

I thought to help her by giving her the amount but then suddenly a second thought came that she would not accept the money from me.

The teacher announced "Students there is a change in the notice, you have to pay only ₹ 1000"

Preeti was now cheering up and my eyes fell on Shweta. She was depressed from the day, I rejected her.

"I want pin drop silence" my class teacher shouted. A very old dialogue that every teacher used to yell in his/her class.

I came home and told my parents about the trip. My father denied to permit me and left for his office. Then I went to my Mom and started helping her, indirectly I was doing chaplusi, so that she permits me, and also she would make papa agree to the trip. My mom was more cunning than me and caught my plan but she permitted me by pulling my ears... She was really a kind-hearted and humble lady.

"Mummy, please make Papa agree to the trip "I requested

"Oh, dear! Just have patience, let your papa come from the office" My mom annoyingly replied.

Papa arrived at 9 p.m. . . . He washed his hands and changed his clothes. We were all in the dining and my mum was waiting for the right moment to talk with papa.

"Hey! Please let Souvik go for the school trip as he is always captured in these four walls. Let him go out and take some fresh air and he will feel relaxed. He will not do any mischief and will also score well in his final exams" My mom signaled me.

Papa again denied but my mother however made him agree to the trip.

That was a very good and extraordinary talent of women, especially my mom's. I however managed for one thousand rupees and handed it over to the teacher with the consent form the very next day. I also saw that Preeti's envelope was also lying on the table. They were almost 21 students who wanted to go on the trip and the rest were not interested because their girlfriends and boyfriends were not going. I was just waiting for the day to arrive so that I can spend quality time with Preeti.

Finally, the day came, it was 19th December 2022, when I was getting ready with my full white shirt and was looking too stylish, energetic, and handsome. We were requested to arrive at the school campus by 8:00 a.m. I reached there half an hour before and there was no one except security guards. We all gathered and there were almost two buses. I wanted to sit with Preeti but Ms.Manju was one of the nose pokers in my love story, she ordered me to sit in another bus. We were all excited to visit Odisha. Shobhit was just sitting behind Preeti and Aditi. I was feeling like pulling Shobhit's hair and throwing him out of the bus. There was a break and the bus stopped at 11 a.m. for some snacks and I slyly changed the bus and sat just behind Preeti.

"Hii Preeti, haven't you bought your snacks" I started the conversation.

"Yes I have bought but I don't feel comfortable eating inside the bus".

"Then give me, I will finish all your tasty snacks" Shobhit giggled.

My cheeks were fully reddened and were just in a mood to slap him hard. He pulled the girl's hair and was laughing. I stood there and slapped him and a fight started inside the bus.

"Stop Souvik" Preeti shouted.

I stopped and Mr.Prakash our P.T teacher, wanted to know the matter. I told him the matter by adding some Mirch Masala in the story.

"Sir, he is intensively pulling the girl's hair and was also trying to insult them"

Mr.Prakash scolded Shobhit and told "Can't you stay decently, wherever you go, some of the other tension is faced by the teachers. Come and sit with me"

We all reached Bhubaneswar and the weather was too captivating and pleasant. My maternal grandfather was a minister of Odisha so we got the hotel rooms at a discount and I also got appreciated by my teachers and friends. We were allotted different rooms and I wanted a room just behind Preeti's room. Preeti was not allotted a room beside me, yes we can predict that it was my bad luck. The hotel was not so luxurious but it was simple and beautiful. Every room was shared among four students. I was sharing the room with Anubhav Manish and Hardik. These three were the most important students in the class. Preeti was sharing the room with Shweta Aditi, Tanisha.

Their group was the epicenter of 'chugli'. Girls should be awarded for this as this was a unique talent found in them.

On that same day at 11 a.m., we were off to the Konark temple and it was interesting to travel on the bus, it was fun learning the fascinating facts about the Konark Temple but I was only interested in Preeti. For the first time, I saw Preeti in a western dress and she was looking damn pretty and hot. Shweta was roaming behind me.

"What happened Shweta?"

"See, you love me or not but I will love you forever" She replied and went running with the queue, which was heading towards the temple. After hearing her, I was like "Uff" and I too joined the boy's queue. In that Temple, our social science teacher Ms. Priya Majumdar taught us about the sculptures which were sculpted on the walls of the temple.

The next day, while we were assembling for the next trip, I was unable to find Preeti. I enquired about her by her two friends and they told me" yes she will be there in a few minutes" in an awkward tone.

She arrived for the trip and her friends told her that I was inquiring about her.

"What's your problem? From the last few days, I am observing that you're just concentrating on me, rather than the school trip"

She blasted on me inside the school bus and all students were looking at me like I did a big crime. I was feeling very ashamed and spectral.

"Don't try to come closer to me, there is no such relationship I want to inbuilt between us rather than a friend." She again yelled

I was depressed, hurt, and was shocked too. Her words attached to my heart, like an arrow to a dartboard.

Anubhav came patting my back and motivated me "Aree bro, leave all these things. Everything will be right soon. Let us enjoy the trip."

I was in shock, so I was crying from within. Everything was flashing back again and again in my mind. It was the worst day of my life. Preeti was one of those, who was too important in my life and her rude act was unpredictable for me. I never wanted to hurt her or I never wished to humiliate her. Still, that day is memorable and makes my goosebumps standstill. I was lost in my world, was not having any breakfast, lunch, snacks, or dinner. Everyone was forcing me but I was not in a mood to eat and enjoy.

That night I went to the garden just near the hotel. I was gazing at the moon and smiled.

Preeti was standing opposite to me and when she turned and saw me, she just left by turning her face. "Preeti.....Pree" I called her but she left.

The next day we planned to cook food for lunch and dinner. The girls were all set and ready to cook and the boys were given the duty to cut vegetables and offer girls. I too chopped some carrots and cabbage and offered it to Preeti. She looked at me and I thought that she would throw the plate and tell "chale jao yahan se" but she accepted the plate with chopped vegetables. After cooking she went to the water basin to wash her hands. I followed her and went to her and before she said something, I apologized and said “Sorry, I am sorry. Preeti my intention was to make you happy, not to humiliate you or make you feel awkward. Just understand my feeling and forget my mistake.

"Don't try to act innocent, Souvik I very well knew what was the intention" she replied in a subconscious voice and left. It was evening time and we all gathered in the nearest park and did a fire camping where we played 'Antakshari'.

It was boys versus girls, we were the first ones to get a chance and the letter was "Ma". The boys started singing and the tune was like a donkey's blabbering.

Now it was the girl's turn and Preeti started, her voice was so sweet and lovely that I felt like Lata Mangeshkar singing in front of me. I clapped and everyone followed me. Her smile was a symbol of forgiveness. The boy's team won the game and we were supposed to give punishment to the girl’s team. The punishment we gave was that - the girls will sing and dance as well.

They tried giving excuses but at last, they started singing and dancing. I was happy to see Preeti dancing. I thought of spending the trip full of excitement, provocations, and excitations but after hearing the hurtful words from Preeti, my trip was in a bad grip.

Shweta and Aditi came to my room. Anubhav was happy seeing Shweta in his room but they came to meet me.

They told me not to lose hope and do my best to make Preeti happy again.

That night itself, at midnight. I made a beautiful card and I was pretty sure that she will be blithe seeing the card.

Slowly, slowly like a thief, I went to the third floor with Anubhav. " I am feeling very scared, if somebody will catch us then we will be thrown from this third floor itself " Anubhav whispered.

"Ha-ha! Don't worry, nothing will happen such as"

I went near Preeti's room and called up Aditi. She opened the door and I went inside and kept the card in Preeti's dressing table. At night too Preeti was looking like a bright star. "Now you leave, if anybody catches you then we will be in a trouble." Aditi intimated in a low tone and we left the room and we saw the security, coming near to us. We started running and he shouted, "Stop ...stop.....chor chor". Everybody's dream and sleep were awakened.

Everyone came out of the rooms. Onto God's grace, we were not caught and everyone told the security that he must have seen something else.

The next morning was a sun-kissed morning with birds chirping and the bells of the temple were rising to a voice. I was curious to know Preeti's reply and when I entered her room, I saw my card torn into pieces and thrown in the dustbin. I left from there with a broken heart. She was not at all looking sad or disconsolate. My tears were not stopping. We were going to visit the Puri sea beach and there I purchased a rose and kept it in Preeti's handbag with a sorry card. She came to me after a few hours, by showing the rose and card she asked: "What is this again and new drama right!?"

"Preeti, I don't want to hurt you. Please forgive me. I am sorry for my mistake."

"Ok, I will forgive you but there is one condition that neither you will talk to me nor you will show your face again."

"Ok if you are happy not talking to me then I will never come to you ".

I went running from there and sat near the pillar and cried a lot. My tears were the pain of my heart.

It was 3 p.m. and was also visited the Puri Jagannath temple the teacher also started teaching about the origin, sculptures, and pilgrimage of the temple.

I was therefore not at all interested to hear her. I was in pain. Everything collapsed and only Preeti was in front of me but it was just a doubt perplexity.

We were returning to the hotel and I found Preeti missing in the bus. I ran from the bus and searched for her.

She fainted in the temple and there was no one to bring her back.

I sprinkled some water on her face but there was no response. I was in a bit tensity and immediately carried her in a trolley which was kept there and admitted her to the nearest clinic. Everyone was searching for Preeti and me. By the time Anubhav informed our teacher that we were in the clinic as Preeti got fainted.

Everyone came there and the teacher asked Preeti "Are you fine dear"

"Yes mam" she replied in a fevered voice.

The doctor said, "Preeti needs some rest and hats off to Souvik that he bought you her and he was without shoes." I also got hurt in my feet as there were some stones and nails which were on the ground. Preeti slapped me and my happy face suddenly turned into a regretted face.

I was a bit confused and she yelled "how dare you carry me in your arms"

"There's some mis....under... " I was replying to her in hesitation and by cutting me she again blasted

"Shut up".

The doctor said "There's some misunderstanding... Souvik bought you in this trolley, not in his arms."

Preeti felt sorry but I was heartbroken and left the clinic and sat inside the bus, in my seat.

That night, in my room I found a box. I opened it and there were some pieces of paper and something was written on it "Sorry ".

I got to know that it was Preeti, who was feeling sorry for her slap. I thought to forgive her mistake as she was more important to me than my self-respect. There were only two days left for the trip. The next day Preeti was talking to me and came close to me and said "Sorry Souvik, I was not supposed to slap you. Please..... Please..... Please... forgive my mistake and I promise you I will be the one who will always be a special friend of yours"

I smiled and said "Human beings are the ones who make mistakes... No worries."

We enjoyed ourselves with the teacher and with my friends as it was the last day of our trip. I would miss the trip a lot as it gave us a lot of memories. We went to many small villages and donated some snacks, rice, and some preferred clothes.

The teacher clicked pictures and we were off to our hotel.

That was the last night in the hotel.

Hardik, Anubhav, Manish, and I planned on scaring the girls. I hung the doll in Preeti's room and Shweta was the first to see the doll and get scared.

She called Tanisha and the doll was too scary to terrify these girls. They yelled and ran out of their rooms. Anubhav and Hardik went into Preeti's room, wearing a black scary face mask and Aditi yelled. Preeti was frightened and the students ran out of their rooms and it was fun scaring them.

Mrs. Manju asked the girls in a frustrating voice "what is wrong with you all? Why are you all shouting?"

"Ma'am there is someone in our room," the girls told in a scowl voice.

We spent the night talking with the teachers and playing interesting games.

Preeti was smiling seeing me as she got to know about our plan and everyone enjoyed the night. We left the next day for Jamshedpur and we took a deep sleep on the bus.

The trip was successful and my bond with Preeti was much stronger now.

WE WERE IN A RELATIONSHIP

Days passed by and we were at the end of class 9. Exams were near and for me, she was the only one, I kept thinking about.

Exams went out like a storm for me as I was not at all prepared for it. Classes passed by, staring at her and I had no idea what the teacher was shouting in the class. We had a break for one month after exams which proved out to be disastrous for me as I started missing Preeti. I often questioned myself that was it love or just attraction?

This question kept me busy for the next few days and finally, the day came when I was promoted to class 10.

On the first day of our session, I reached before time just to see Preeti but was unable to find her. I went into the class and sat where she used to sit during class 9.

I waited and kept waiting but she didn't come to the class the whole day. I was getting into depression each day and wish to see her once.

I never realized when she became a drug for me, it was only "her" I needed at that moment.

On the third day, I was out of control and directly went to her friends and enquired about her.

They do give me weird looks but I got my answer as well which was more important than that looks. She was not in the town and went to Ranchi to attend a wedding and she will be joining classes the day after tomorrow. I collected all love songs and imagined Preeti with me. The next day when I entered my class someone called me from the back.

"Souvik"

I looked back and it was Preeti who was calling me and I was on the ninth cloud.

"Yes" I replied

"Why were you inquiring about me?"

I had goosebumps at that time and a feeling of fear aroused in me.

"You weren't in the class for many days," I replied in a cool manner.

"Ummmm..."

She smiled and made a suspicious expression on her face. I was unable to understand her. As I told you earlier, understanding girls was a big threat for me. The same night I got a call and the number was flashing 984*******.

I received the call and spoke up "Hello".

There was a sweet voice on the other side and she too told "Hello Souvik ".

"Yes, who are you?"

"I am Preeti here"

I was so happy at that moment as if I received a Padma Shri award.

"Yes... ye...yes, how can I help you?"

“I just wanted to know will you come to school tomorrow."

"Yes, I will come"

"Ok bye"

"Hello.....Hel.....For what?" But the call was hung up.

I was so fortunate after her call that I sang the whole day.

"Ho ek ladki ko dekha to aisa laga,

Ek ladki ko dekha to aisa laga

Jaise khilta gulaab

Jaise shaayar ka khwaab

Jaise ujli kiran

Jaise van mein hiran

Jaise chaandni raat

Jaise naghme ki baat

Jaise mandir mein ho ek jalta diya

Ho ek ladki ko dekha to aisa laga"

My sister Shruti was hearing me and suddenly she knocked on the door and my romantic mood was in the drain.

“Is this song written in your books?"

“What?" I questioned in an annoying voice.

"Idiot, I mean to say that why are you singing these songs? .... it is the time to study not to sing"

She gave a lecture for 10 minutes and her repeated dialogue was “padhoge likhoge banoge Nawab , kheloge koodoge banoge kharab."

I just felt like, somebody is now a villain of my love story.

The next day, I was curious to know why Preeti had called me the last night.

I sat on my bench and waited for Preeti to arrive. She entered the classroom and her eyes were on me.

Just after her, Shweta entered and her eyes were also on me.

I was in fear that, has Preeti complained to anyone about me that I am always after her.

But I was wrong, Preeti had given my name in the annual day function.

We had to perform a natak and she was also a part of it.

I told to myself “girls are always experts in doing Natak''.

My heart went on "Udi udi jaye,

Udi udi jaye

Dil ki patang dekho

Udi udi jaye".

Still, I had a dubiety in my mind that why Shweta was staring at me? Yaa, I was her pehla pyaar.

For the annual day function, I challenged my friends that I would propose Preeti and would tell her my feelings for her, but I was scared from within.

I was tensed, not for the challenge but the fear of rejection was giving severe pain to my heart. We started practicing for the natak and it was a fun-filled day with my friends. I was the kind of person who never loved seeing people in a sad mood. While we were practicing for the skit, everyone judged me, some called me 'funny bhaiya', some called me 'joker', some called me 'comedian' and some call me the 'entertainer'. I was happy to get different designations from my classmates, juniors, and seniors. I wanted to see a smile on Preeti's face and I was successful in bringing a smile.

Her smile was too erotic and addictive.

My heart started "Has mat pagli, pyaar ho jayega" .

Everyone loved my jokes and comments but my full focus was on Preeti's smile as somewhere I heard that girls get impressed by the person who makes them laugh the most.

While practicing for the skit, one girl named Sanam, fell for me.

Yes, you guessed it right. She was in love with me and proposed to me the same night when I planned to propose Preeti.

"Souvik, I love you, not because you are handsome, but you are so good from the core of your heart."

"Sanam, please try to understand, I can't be in a relationship with you because I love someone else"

For her, it was like a storm hitting her and again I hurt someone.

Hurting someone was not my fault, if someone loves me it doesn't mean that I too love her.

"The girl whom you love is the luckiest one but do remember, I will a good friend of yours"

Sanam repeated the same as Shweta did.

I was in a bit hurry so that Preeti doesn't leave the function. It was gloomy weather in the evening and I was in search of Preeti for the past 15 minutes.

My eyes were on the brake when I saw a Preeti dressing up for the function, in one of the classrooms.

Her dressing made me mad for her.

When I saw her, I felt like hugging her and declaring that I love her. But I was hesitating in telling her that. I knocked on the door, Preeti gave a broad smile seeing me.

"Oh! Come on Souvik"

"Thank you"

I was continuously looking at Preeti. At that moment I thought that Preeti was the most beautiful, charming, hot, stylish, glossy, bold, Stunner.............. And the list goes on...

"Hey! What are you dreaming?" She shook me.

“Oh sorry! Actually, I wanted to tell you something"

“yes tell" she replied by setting up her chunni.

I closed my eyes and told her “I ......I...love you"

When I opened my eyes, I saw that she was staring at me. She left the room crying. I was scared and my heartbeat was rising to the highest level.

I too left the room and we were called for the last rehearsals of our Natak which was based on "Acid attack".

One girl came running to me and told me to meet Preeti urgently. At that moment my expressions were such, that can't be expressed in words.

She was gazing at the clock and it seemed that she was waiting for me. I went inside and she offered a seat. She came near to me and I was finger crossed. I thought that she would kiss me but she came near to my face and whispered in my ears “I love you too". Preeti ran from the room and I was shocked hearing this.

The natak ended and we were successful in doing that.

Our teachers praised us but I was least bothered. I was just in love with the words" I love you too" which Preeti told me in my ears. The next day was Sunday and we chatted for almost half an hour. It was the first time when I was very much excited for Monday. I reached the school and I saw Preeti standing with friends. She gave a broad smile seeing me and my reaction was always a smile. My Monday was spent very happily and I gave all the answers asked by my teachers.

At that moment, I was the most felicitous person in the world.

Everything was happening to me, like a dream. Proposing her and being in a relationship with Preeti was a dream coming true for me, but on that day what happened with her was just out of my thinking.

We usually call each other after reaching our home but on that day, I was waiting for her call.

One hour, two hours, three hours, and the whole day passed. It was evening now and I was a bit strained. I thought that if she has forgotten to call me. Being a true lover of hers, I called up at 8 p.m. and as the tring-tring was increasing my tension was changing into curiosity. "The number you have called is currently busy, please call again later". The call was cut.

I was confused that why Preeti declined my call.

That night went to sleeplessness and full of tension.

The next day, I ran for the school and asked her friends about Preeti, and the news they gave me made my day worst. I jumped the school boundary and ran to the main Hospital where she was admitted.

Preeti met an accident and hearing it, made me cry but my eyes held my tears. When I entered the hospital, I went towards the reception and got to know that she was admitted to the ICU. While running towards the ICU, I fell on the stairs got a severe hurt on my forehead, and was unable to stand. A crowd gathered to gossip about me but nobody was ready to take me to the doctor. However, I stood up and ran towards the ICU and saw Preeti's family over there and if they would see me then it would lead to great trouble for me and of course for Preeti.

Her mother was crying and the pain of her father was noticeable on his face. I was not getting any idea that how to meet Preeti. I dressed up as a nurse and was looking pretty hot. I went to the ICU and suddenly Preeti's mother stopped me and she noticed my leg hairs. I turned and started the conversation with a female voice. "Why are there so many hairs in your leg?"

"Mummy ji......." Oh! Shit, what I told made everyone astonished.

"What mummy Ji" she auspiciously queried

"Oh! Sorry aunty Ji, actually my mother also looks like you, so that's why....... by the way it's my childhood problem. I have leg hairs from my childhood."

She noticed something on my face but I was wearing a mask and she requested me to pull over my mask from my face.

"Aunty Ji, the patient is serious, and I have to leave. Sorry."

I went into the ICU and cried a lot seeing Preeti.

She was lying on the bed and I held her hands. She saw me and tears rolled down her cheeks. She felt better seeing me and a smile was flashing. I give them a supportive hand to her hand and was about to leave the room. She held my hands like a romantic film scene. I gave her a passport size photograph of mine, which was in my wallet and I left the room. Unexpectedly, my nurse cap fell and a drama scene was created. Preeti's family was astonished seeing me and they called up the security to catch me but I jumped, swung, and did all gymnast and ran from the hospital. I went home and there was a surprise for me as I met my maternal grandfather after a long time. I hugged him and chit chat with him for more than an hour. My Nanaji was a businessman who was a well-known person in the city.

On that same day, my Nanaji fell from the stairs and suffered a lot. My grandfather taunted me and said "You are a bad omen for everyone, whosoever you meet, the person is in trouble. Three years back, it was your grandmother and now your maternal grandfather."

Yes, my grandmother. My both grandparents used to live in Bombay. As my grandfather was a retired police officer and my grandmother was a businesswoman she loved me the most. After a long time, she came to meet me. The next day she lost her life due to a heart attack and my grandfather believes that it was because of me as I was a bad omen for her.

I was in depression for a few days as I thought about Preeti.

My grandfather's words were like an arrow hitting my heart and all his lines were repeated one by one in my mind again and again.

I fainted and immediately my parents inducted me in the hospital where Preeti was admitted. My mom was just praying for my welfare but it was nothing such dangerous or serious with me. My blood pressure was low and I faced weakness.

I was only and solely thinking about my grandfather's words. I thought that I was a bad omen for everyone as whosoever loved me, falls in affliction. I prayed to God.

“Oh, God! Please cure Preeti and I promise that I will never talk to her" I always wanted the sake and welfare of Preeti and I never wished to lose her.

After a few hours, I was discharged from the hospital and didn't attend school. If I would attend the school then I would haven't gained control over myself, to talk to Preeti.

We were not the weakness but the strength of each other. I had faith in our true love that it will never separate. But true love faces the most number of problems.

23rd June 2024: Preeti ranged me twice but giving a pause to my love and emotion, I block her number from my contact list.

Her messages made my heart cry. Her smile, her way of turning towards me, her way of walking, and everything of hers was flashing back and was unable to find a way to get back from all of these. My friends {Hardik, Manushi

(Hardik's Girlfriend) Aditi, Anubhav, and specifically Preeti} were worried about me.

The most worried person was Shweta as I was her first love.

Their calls were ringing to me simultaneously but I didn't answer any of the calls.

To know the matter, Hardik and Anubhav came to my house in search of me. I was on my balcony gazing at the mountains and the kites which were changing the directions like my life. Hardik and Anubhav entered through the main gate and it amazed me. I went to my mom and said that if any inquires about me, then to tell them that I am out of town.

My mom before asking me anything ran to my room.

Hardik and Anubhav greeted my mom with "Namaste aunty Ji". My mom requested Mr. Ravi (our servant) to bring some cold drinks for them. I was hiding and was looking at them.

"Aunty where is Souvik?" They inquired about me by looking at my house at 360 degrees.

"Beta, he is out of town to attend a wedding" my mom hesitated while telling this lie. They drank the cold drink and left. While they were leaving my house, I was hiding on my balcony looking at them and they saw me from the rear mirror of the bike which was parked on the lawn. Unknowingly, they went out of the gate. The moment, I went inside my room, they again entered like a spy. Without making any sound of their feet, they entered my room through the ladder and I was speechless seeing them. They entered my room by clapping like a filmy scene or like the Saas-Bahu serial.

They hugged me tightly and started questioning me a lot.

I narrated the whole story but they thought my grandfather's words to be debris and rubbish.

They planned to reframe our love story. Preeti's sister Naina also got to know about our relationship and rather than being angry, she was happy getting such a handsome, sweet, kind, humorous, and talented Jijaji.

Naina also played a very lead role in our love story by supporting us. Our exams were near and we were instructed to fill out the form for our examination. My friends planned to get Preeti and me together again. I too came to fill the form but in a disguised form by wearing the cap and applying goggles.

One boy came running towards me and pushed me and said "sorry bhaiya", but my goggles fell and were broken.

I shouted "Oh no!".

Everybody gazed at me as I did on offense. Preeti too saw me and she was blithe seeing me. She came running towards me like Kajol came running for Shahrukh in DDLJ.

She questioned me "Souvik, where were you from last few days?"

"Aa...Actually....."

"Is there anything personal..?Don't feel shy to share with me"

I ran from there. She called "Souvik....listen......Souvik "but I went wiping my tears.

I assume that she must be thinking that "Mujhe chhodkar, Jo Tum jaaoge ,bada pachtaoge ,bada pachtaoge"

She went to Hardik and Anubhav for succor and requested them to find out the reason behind my depression.

They both looked at each Other as they were knowing the whole depression story. Hardik was the one who couldn't store any news and he just vomited everything, which was told by me. Preeti was amused and she wanted to meet me urgently. Usually, we meet in a temple but this time I rejected to meet her as I wanted her to be in a good condition. He called me from Anubhav's number and as soon as I picked up the call, she gave me the oath to meet her in the temple.

We both reached the temple but I was staying apart from her and the moment I came closer to her, a small thorn came under her foot and the bitter lines of my grandfather got repeated in my mind again. I helped Preeti to get out of the pain, which the thorn gave her, and was about to leave the place, without talking to her. By the time, I was about to leave, she held my hand and pulled me towards the bench.

We both sat there and Preeti hugged me and said" Souvik, The thing which your grandfather told are not at all true.

We are tied in a bond of love and whatever took place with me, was just a coincidence. You are not a bad omen for me, though you are my lucky charm and without you, my life is blank and vacuous. All the gestures you did for me, became a moment. Remember, that day when I was admitted to the hospital I was senseless. The moment you held my hand my senses were back. Think how black would be our life if we stay apart and I also know that you are too feeling the same as me. I hope you understand"

I was highly motivated by her words and emotions. At that time I was really in a doubt.....that is she Sandeep Maheshwari's daughter?

I held her hands and nodded my head upside down. We were again together. I unblocked her and our chatting was again on the track. I was happily back into our relationship but the circumstances I faced later, you would know in later chapters.

COLLEGE LIFE

It was the time for our 12th board, the most deadly and somber examination.

Preeti's presence did wonders to my life. There was an announcement to be announced in the class and Preeti being the monitor was supposed to announce. She came in front of the class and her style of announcing the notice was too sensational. I felt like Neha Kakkar was performing in front of me. The bell ranged and we were dispersed. Preeti was standing near the gate and was waiting for her mom or dad to pick her up, meanwhile, I went to her and closed her eyes, and gave her a beautiful pendant in which S&P was grated. She loved the pendant and gave a kiss to the pendant. I was feeling jealous towards the pendant and wished she would kiss me too.

There were some children playing basketball and the ball came flying towards Preeti and I stopped the ball. She was safe but my hand got rashes. The moment, I went to give them the ball and scold them, Preeti's mom arrived and I felt like touching her feet as she would be my future mother-in-law.

I too went home after Preeti left. I prepared for my board examination and there were only two days left for my exams. As the days were near, my tension was raising the most.

Finally, the day came to appear for the board exams, and on that day, I went to all the temples in Jamshedpur. It's a very interesting and funny fact that whenever we are in trouble or we face any problem we first remember God.

20th May 2025: That day I was at a very low ebb as I completed my 12th board exams and finally the day came to leave our school. I scored 90% and it was a big achievement for me and my family. Preeti too scored well but much better than me. She scored 95% and as expected she was the district topper.

Finally, the day came for our farewell and besides my sadness, I was glad too. I was glad owing to, I will see Priti in saree for the first time. I was confident with my thought, that she must be looking hot and soothing with the saree look.

It was almost time but I was unable to find her. At that same moment, I saw something very glancing, attractive, and shiny.

There was a girl dressed up with red velvet saree but she was turned back, and I was impotent to her.

One of her friends called "Preeti" and she turned towards me. My reaction was like OMG... She was looking too pretty. Her deep black eyes, her shiny pendant, her stylish bracelet, and the way she was tucking her hair behind her ears, made me a fan of her beauty. It was not that, I was looking dumb. I was to look you unique and handsome with my fine glazing blazer.

Hardik after seeing Preeti uttered "She is looking like an atom bomb"

I tapped his head and told "Abae Teri bhabhi h"

With the royal and dashing walk, I went towards Preeti and she excused her friends to talk to me.

I told "Your look stole my heart. You are looking gorgeous"

"You are too looking handsome Souvik"

We were holding each other's hands and our PT Teacher Mr. Pradeep saw us but I was astonished to see his reaction. He told us in a romantic voice "Hota hai, Hota hai, Pyar Mein sab Kuch chalta Hai".

It was time for the function, Preeti and I sat close to each other's chairs. Our hostess Ms. Rashi was looking glamorous and peppery. I was continuously gazing at her and Preeti tapped on my back and told "Yes...yes....you only gaze at her. What is so special about her? She is just wearing a western dress and if I too wear it, I challenge you, I will look much hotter than her...

" Haha, you are being jealous" I jokingly uttered.

"Just shut up".She replied.

Preeti was a kind-hearted and innocent girl and those were some qualities that made me her fan too.

Many got awarded for their skills and talent. Preeti and I were also one of them. Though it was the last day of our school there were many such memories combined with my school.

I was so thankful to my school for giving me memories and Preeti.

Preeti was my first and last love. She guided me more than a girlfriend, she never tried to use me rather she always helped me out whenever I needed her.

It was time for us to leave the school and give a final goodbye. I went to the washroom as it was a bit urgent.

The security guards were unknown that I was in the washroom and they locked the building and switched off the lights. My work was in progress very smoothly in the washroom and suddenly when the lights went off, I was scared. I shouted for help "Who is there? Help me out"

The building door was locked and there was no one to listen to me. I was just roaming in that particular building like a ghost.

It was a chilled night and I was in search of a better place to sleep but the doors were locked. I was feeling lonely and I was being horrified. When I used to read in primary classes, a rumour was accustomed to spreading that our library teacher, Ms. Lata committed suicide in the library and her spirit is still alive in the school. After the deadly conception arose in my mind, I saw a shadow that passed through our school Garden.

I was just chatting "Jai Hanuman Gyan gun Sagar.......".

Hanuman Chalisa was the best cure during these situations.

Slowly, without making any footsteps I went to the top floor of the building to see who was there behind the shadow. It was daring to see that there were two shadows indeed and both of them were nodding their head. It may seem funny but at that time it was a bursting situation for me. While I came down the stairs, the shadow was coming nearer to me.

"Oh God! Save me, mummy"...

Again I ran upstairs and sat near the biology lab.

Sweat was dripping continuously the building's door was opening slowly and someone entered the building.

The shadow came upstairs by dragging its feet. I ran from the biology lab and went towards the water filter.

I left my hometown on 23rd July 2026 for my graduation. This was the first time I was traveling alone and that too Bombay. My mother and father came to drop me at the station. I had mixed feelings and emotions when I boarded the train. I knew my mom was very sad as she didn't want me to leave her and go so far. She had tears in her eyes but somehow she didn't want me to see it.

In those days I got to know that we are living in the 21st century, and it's not only girls who leave their parents and go but boys too leave their parents to live their dreams.

Today every student wants to study in a good institution, get better knowledge and education. And almost 90% of cities lack good colleges. Thus everyone leaves one's city for higher education, job opportunities, etc. I feel those students are lucky who get the chance to live with their parents.

Unlike us, who leave everything behind, sacrifice almost everything just to live their dreams and have a better life.

So I watched my mother, standing helpless on the platform, while the train moved for the next destination. The sight got dimmer and finally, I went inside.

College life: the freedom, the sense of being grown-up, and responsibility of us on our shoulders! College life prepares us for the big bad world that lies ahead. We learn a lot about ourselves and fellow homo-sapiens while living on our own in the dorms and hostels. Another interesting aspect of college life is certain discoveries and improvisations that we make while we are on our own and find ourselves in a difficult situation.

The next day was a very serene day for me. It was a bright Monday morning. I made my breakfast and went for a shower. I gulped down the scrambled eggs and toast and quickly wore my black t-shirt and jeans as I was being late for my college.

When you are late, God always had some special games to play with you. I ran downstairs as quickly as I could, almost falling twice but finally managing it. I found my bike punctured there and out of anger I kicked the tire and hurt myself. I ran to catch an auto-rickshaw but none was willing to go to my college. All refuse due to the big jam in that part of the city. I tried to convince them but everyone denied it. After trying for 15 minutes, I gave up booking a cab and headed towards my destination.

Yes, there was a huge traffic jam near my college.

It hardly takes 15 minutes to reach there but it took almost half an hour that day. I was unhappy, frustrated, and tired. I reached 40 minutes late to my classroom and physics Professor Mr. Jai Prakash scolded me and told me to stand outside. Preeti Hardik, Aditi, Anubhav, Manushi, and I took admission to the same college in Bombay.

In the next period, I went to my classroom and sat near Preeti and the first day of college was spent cheerful and frustrating.

I was getting bored in the evening and decided to change the boring Monday evening and go out shopping with Preeti. I like being busy, I am extremely workaholic and sometimes I even get sick because of sleeping less. I was not a shopping kind of guy but I had to get some new clothes which have now become a necessity. I didn't want my jeans to tear in the wrong situation. Preeti and I went to the Oberoi mall, which is one of the famous malls in Mumbai. It is known for its fascinating dresses, cafes, bars restaurants, and pubs.

We went to four outlets and bought some clothes. By that time Hardik, Anubhav, Manushi, and Aditi arrived. Anubhav was a bit stingy when it comes to spending money but I gave him two new t-shirts as a gift as I also worked as a content writer and earned approximately 20,000 per month. I also gifted Preeti with one stunning jacket and beautiful jeans. I bought a couple of pairs of jeans, two black t-shirts, a goggle, and a blue full sleeve check shirt. We also planned to have our dinner in the cafe. We ordered Biryani, prawn rice, and chili chicken. Hardik and I both loved having chicken. Anubhav was sweating in the heat and I somehow managed to gulp down the chili chicken. Mumbai Cafe has the hottest and the spiciest chili chicken in the town. When you order chili chicken, you get CHILLI chicken.

We somehow managed to eat our dinner and headed towards the parking. It took around 5 minutes to reach theirs. Aditi paid the parking charges and I went to take my motorcycle. Preeti, Anubhav, Hardik, and Manushi are planning to book a cab for themselves but I denied and request Preeti to come and sit behind me. It was being so romantic like an Arijit Singh album. She placed her hand on my shoulders and her hair was flowing with air which I could see in my bike's mirror. We all lived in the same hostel. I was tired, impatient, and kind of thirsty. I just wanted to go home and sleep. It was the second day of my college and I also filled a form in the Maddock Film Production for my auditions which were scheduled on 15th September 2026. I was also interested in acting.

I bunked half of my classes as I also took coaching to clear UPSC exams. At noon my father called me and I sensed that one of his 'Gyan sessions' was about to start. Souvik, you have to study seriously. You are at a very critical juncture of life you have to handle everything by yourself from now onwards. No cigarettes, no alcohol, no bad company, and no girlfriends. You are my only hope"

"Ok Papa" I nodded, although I knew I would not follow 70% of his instructions I said this to stop him from repeating his old refrain. The day however he was unstoppable and at last he told "Remember beta, you are my brave son". With those inspiring words, he hung up the call.

My content writing job was a typical online job from 6 p.m. to 9 p.m. and like usual it was killing me from inside.

But as I was good in writing skills, some days went far better. But I was mostly irritated by the bullshit BOSS who came game between our sessions and I was his target for the scolding. The next day I got a chance to examine the college, the college students, and staff. There were around 30 students busy filling up some forms. I went to that lady who was distributing that form. I inquired about the form and she gently explained what to fill in.

She was beautiful, young, and had a charismatic personality.

She was unmarried and looked hardly 25. I later came to know, she was one of our faculties. Her name was Sheela Dutta and still, she's one of my favourite teachers.

Apart from admiring her in the room, there were many other beautiful girls in the room. Yes, the Mumbai girls have something in themselves. They had an appealing personality and a good sense of dressing, some had multi-highlight whereas some had temporary curls, and some wore high heels whereas some wore canvas shoes. The boys were stylish and were properly grooved. In short, everyone looked wonderful. This is one of the things which big cities have but I was only for Preeti and only for her.

Why I came to my bench, Preeti gave a small chit, there it was written that I was looking handsome and some girls behind Preeti were discussing me. A shy kind of feeling occurred but still, I was proud of my appearance.......

As in school, I rejected the two girls and now it was time to reject the ones who tried to propose to me in college.

I am a new friend there. My group and I went to Red rose restaurant which was just next to the college and we were served with Coca-Cola and two pieces of samosa each costing rupees 9. Yes, it was costly as in Jamshedpur it usually never rises above rupees 7.

I generally gave treats to my friends and this time too I paid the bill.

23rd September 2026: I was ready to give my auditions and none of my friends even Preeti knew about this. I went to the production house and so many youngsters were on the way to follow their dreams as Mumbai was a city of Dreams. It was a big race for me and if I would have stepped back then it would have been a great situation of demise.

After waiting for an hour, it was my chance and I submitted some of my photographs. They started clicking my profiles and the word 'ACTION' raised my heartbeat and made me nervous.

I started acting and the result would be declared after 7 days.

After 7 days, I went to the production house and I was rejected. This happened to me several times.

“This acting field is not made for me," I told to myself. That day was spent in depression and I was not in a mood to answer any of my friend's questions. Once while focusing on my content writing job, I got an opportunity to write for an Ad- film and the director loved my writing skills.

The ad was telecasted and I got well paid for my writing the director Shri Mani Ratnam also loved my acting which he saw me trying in front of the mirror.

Life was unpredictable and I got a chance to work in a pressure cooker advertisement that would be telecasted nationwide. It was happening so rapidly that I didn't have time, even to inform my family and friends.

4th October 2026: My ad was cast on the television and everyone was shocked seeing me on the screen. Preeti came running to my room and hugged me. She was happier than ever.

"Wow, it seems so lucky to have a boyfriend, who is on television..Haha".

I was speechless and smiled seeing Preeti's excitement.

My phone started ringing and I felt like a busy celebrity. Hardik and Anubuav were out for shopping and they saw me on the television in the mall and came running to give me wishes. Aditi and Manushi bought a bouquet for me and the moment was a moment of dancing and cheering. In my hostel, everyone was waiting to get pictures clicked with me. As soon as I went outside for ice cream, the ice-cream seller exclaimed "It seems that I have seen you somewhere"

Anubhav told "Aree.... you must have seen him in the pressure cooker ad"

"Oh yes .....Sir, please give me your autograph"

He also clicked some selfies with me and gave me one free ice cream. My parents were also getting praised. Life took a sudden change and I also got a known face in my college.

PREETI COMMITTED SUICIDE

Aditi came running to me and she was being panic. I was tense seeing her.

"Preeti has jumped from balcony surprised to me in a crying tone I ran downstairs, crying and wiping my tears. I saw blood was rolling down her head. I carried her in my arms and ran towards the nearby hospital. The doctor admitted Preeti to the ICU as it was an emergency case. I prayed to God for her recovery. The nurse wasn't sure about her life. Hardik, Anubhav, and Manushi arrived to give me strength. Preeti was still in the bed, with no sense and no movement. After waiting for more than an hour, the doctor came and informed us about Preeti's condition. He is not sure about her health. "She might fall in a coma or she might die" he sadly informed.

I was broken and broken. I went to her and cried a lot...

“You didn't care about me, even a single time. How can I live without you, have you ever thought about this? You are only the starting and end of my life. You are my life and only you. The journey is blank without you, just once wake up. If you die then I will lose everything." crying continuously I told.

I was about to leave and a miracle took place. Preeti's hand and legs were moving a bit.

The Doctor, after some treatment, told us that she was out of danger and she will be discharged after 10 to 15 days of rest.

"There has to be someone with her, to take care of her". I requested to stay with Preeti and advised my friends to go back. After 10 to 15 days of bedridden, we were back to our hostel. Preeti's condition was far better and this was the time to ask Preeti why she took this kind of step.

We reached our rooms Preeti hugged me and cried a lot. "I have never seen such a person like you. Caring, funny, romantic, and everything. Thank you for being in my life".

I was willing to ask her the reason behind the incident but as instructed by the doctor, I was not allowed to give her any kind of stress or rigidity. I also notified her friends, not to ask her any kind of question. A couple of weeks passed and I thought of asking Preeti why she took such a dangerous step. I knocked on the door. Manushi opened the door and I was curious to talk to Preeti. She was in the bathroom taking a bath. I waited for her impatiently, cracked some jokes to make Manushi laugh. She went outside for a while.

A helping sound came from the bathroom.

“Manushi can you please give me the towel which is on the bed"

I searched for Manushi here and there but couldn't find her. I took the towel and when she opened the bathroom door and saw me, she banged the door and asked in a very awkward and shameful tone 'what are you doing here?'

I hesitated and told "actually, I came to talk to you but you were not present so I was waiting for you"

"Oh...... ok"

She forwarded her hands for the towel and I directly gave her the towel without making the scene romantic. Preeti came out of the bathroom and she was looking damn racy and provocative. By seeing her, q short and romantic Shayari popped up in my mind.

"Main fannah ho gya uski ek jhalak Dekhkar

Na Jane roz aayene par kya gujarti hogi."

She was looking a bit upset.

"Preeti, can you please take the pain of telling me why you took such a great step?"

She avoided me and started combing her hair.

"I am asking you something"

"I don't want to discuss anything about this" with those words, she was about to leave for college. I holded her and pulled her back.

She started crying and clasped me. I was totally in confusion and what to utter was out of my mind.

“Stop crying and tell me, what is the matter?"

"While we were out shopping, Shobhit (who was always jealous of Preeti and me) has attached a hidden camera in our bathroom and everything has been captured in it, not only mine but Aditi and Manushi too.

"What! He had made an MMS" I burst like an atom bomb.

Manushi entered the room and the vegetables which she was carrying with her, fell from her hand. She heard everything and fainted. We both tried to handle her. I called Hardik, Aditi, and Anubhav and requested them to meet urgently in my room.

We all gathered but I was the one who was out of control.

I narrated everything to them.

Everyone was astonished.

After a few minutes of discussion, Shobhit called Preeti, we told her to pick up the call.

'Hello Preeti" He whispered like a villain.

'You bloody, Chut*****... " I blasted on him.

"Chup! You know that whatever I have with me is very dangerous for your love, Souvik. If you want that I should delete it, then tell Preeti to come to my room but before coming to my room, she should break up with you. If you don't agree with my wish then that may be harmful to you and the MMS would be globally approved ... Ha...ha...ha...."

I was out of control after hearing him and was about to hit him hard. There was a twist in the scene.

Aditi with sarcastic fear told, "Actually, I have enabled call recording in Preeti's phone two days back"

Preeti amusingly said, "Why so?"

"Actually I wanted to hear, what Souvik and you talked late at night. The romantic Shayari, the funny jokes and the lovely talks to you did"

“it’s very bad Aditi........"

Preeti's scolding session went never to an end. I stopped Preeti and praised Aditi for her work as the recording will help us as a shred of big evidence.

We planned something and worked on it. In the evening Anubhav dressed as a hotel waiter, and entered Shobhit's room. Shobhit was sharing his room with Piyush, Ravi, and Prince. Anubhav mixed sleeping tablets in their coffee and left the room. Anubhav was disguised in such a way that made him look like a gentleman.

After a while, we all entered his room with the police officer and started searching for the MMS file. We were unable to find it. The Inspector Sushant Rao role was too in search of that.

While we were in search of the MMS, Pradeep was back with sense and he was in fear seeing the police with us. Mr. Sushant howled at him asking "where is the MMS"

"Sir I don't have any MMS..... Please spare me"

Then by turning on the recording here again investigated "Then what is this?"

Shobhit hesitated. "Tell the truth" the inspector roared on him like Singham.

Sir don't hit me. I am telling the truth actually I was very irritated from their relationship and friendship. I wanted to put them in trouble and bother them a lot. I planned about this but believe me, sir, I haven't made any MMS.

The inspector nodded and investigated his cell, laptop, and the whole room. Shobhit was saved but as we have registered an FIR, he has to be in the lockup for disturbing the public, due to which Preeti could have lost her life.

I too was annoyed by Preeti's behaviour and told her in a frustrated voice "Preeti, you should have been concerned about this, with me. Don't take any such step which will trouble me and your family"

"Sorry.. Sorry...Souvik and all my friends"

I was happy getting her back with me, in a good condition, and thanked God for saving her.

Again, we were back to our college days. The tallest boy Kartik was made to sit on the first bench by our English teacher for some obvious reason. It was during an English class, the teacher was teaching us a lesson. She suddenly notices Kartik sitting comfortably on the first bench and reading a novel "One night at the call center".

On being asked by the teacher as to why he wasn't falling what was being taught, he confesses that he hasn't got the book for the the particular subject as it was compulsory to carry all those books which were mentioned on the timetable.

The teacher turns to the class and explains in explain am "Look at this fellow, sitting on the first bench, and does not even care to inform you that he has not brought his book. That too, this shameless is reading this kind of novel in the classroom."

Kartik replied in a very innocent tone" Actually mam, I thought that I should not disturb the class while you are teaching." The class burst into laughter and the teacher could not control her smile either.

Time moved like a bullet train, everything was passing on so quickly. The lectures started to get boring but college life was becoming more interesting because of my friends.

Exams were near and so was Preeti's birthday. I had been planning to give a big surprise since June. Her birthday was on August 5 and exams were to begin on 12th August. I was the last night preparing student and never studied beforehand. On either hand, Preeti was very studious nowadays and mature too. She was already done with the syllabus and was ready for the exams. Everyone had ideas.

We chose the best idea and planned a very unique surprise for her.

We all planned not to wish at the midnight and won't even talk to her. We would pretend to forget her birthday and we all knew that she would get angry.

We all switched off her room light and I was dressed in very terrifying and scary clothes and was about to scare Preeti. She gave me one punch, two kicks, and five slaps rather than getting scared. Then everyone switched on the lights and sang for her. I was dumped in that corner as I was suffering from pain and was in a very bad condition.

"Where is Souvik" Preeti curiously questioned.

"The person whom you punched, kicked, and slapped is none other than Souvik," Anubhav told.

"OMG.....Souvik gets up...."

My all heropanti was in a drain but I was happy seeing Preeti's happy face.

"Let's cut the cake," said Preeti.

We had our dinner, clicked some pictures, and had a brief discussion about the upcoming exams. Soon it was time for us to leave. I gave Preeti a bracelet and said 'this is for you, I hope you like it.

"You are so sweet" She blushed. Our exam got over on 23rd August and we had a holiday cum break of three weeks.

Everyone went home and so did I. There were no classes and there was no reason for me to stay in Mumbai. I went home after a long gap of 11 months. It was the longest time I stayed away from my family. I reached Jamshedpur in the early evening. This time something was different at my house. I was treated differently, everyone was nice to me even my father who used to trash and scold me. I was treated like a VIP. I thought of talking about Preeti with my mother but I was in a fear of rejection.

Three weeks passed like a storm and I didn't get any right time to tell my parents about Preeti. This was our last year in college and then where would life land us was unpredictable.

I was eager to participate in every activity of my college and I won prizes for debate, sports and natak. I always had a wish to sing in front of everybody and get everybody's applause. Then one fine day I gave my name to be included in that list of singers. I thought everybody enjoyed my singing but to my surprise, they gave a lot of chits in which it was written: *"Tumhe to Koyal samjha tha, tum to kouwa nikle yaar"*strictly warning me not to sing again. This incident was a memorable one for me and I would never forget it in my life.

Days went quickly and her final year exam begin. It was a hot afternoon in the month of May and we were completely exhausted sitting for three hours in the examination hall without an air conditioner. Some students even converted their question papers into a hand fan.

I completed my paper and does had to sit idle for an hour more.

There was a myth in our university that the more you fill the paper, the more marks you get.

While everyone was living that myth, I was busy counting the number of crows in the tree.

Another favorite time pass was to stare at Preeti. Her hair attracted me every time. She used to pay extra attention to the presentation of a paper. She used to draw margins on both sides of the paper. The next day was an extra class of chemistry and we three (Hardik Anubhav and I) bunked the class. We went to the nearby cinema hall and Anubhav sat near a girl who was quite pretty. We had a gala time watching the movie in the theatre. I purchase samosa, popcorn, and cola. Hardik paid the ticket fare. As I told you earlier, Anubhav was a bit stingy in spending money.

We returned to our classrooms after the break and I went to our Maths professor Ms. Nisha and I discussed the farewell party. Third-year students were responsible for the farewell party. Everything was planned but the only thing which bothered us was the budget. Our college was very hand-fisted and never gave a good budget for the farewell.

But we were confident that we would get the desired amount from the administration as we knew them personally. We wrote an application and all expenses in detail and went to talk to the administrative head. They accepted and then told that for a farewell party the college can give some amount of funds as it was important for the college's reputation.

We took permission for the farewell party at the campus. The college gave us a very low fund which was around 6000 to 8000 only. "How will you get the fund," asked Anubhav.

"Yes it will cost more than 30,000 rupees"

"From where will you arrange that money?" added Aditi

"We will contribute and ask our other classmates to contribute 500 each, then we can easily accumulate more than 30000 rupees as we are 62 in strength".

"Are you out of mind, no one will contribute? I can guarantee you that" Anubhav said.

"You all are paying, right?" I asked

"Of course, we will contribute but what about the rest of them?" asked Preeti.

"I will talk to them" I replied.

I spoke to the class during the lunch break. A few agreed whereas a few didn't.

Around 35 people said yes including six of us. We were still short of money.

We totally collected 25,500. Our teacher Ms. Priya also contributed Rupees 1500 for our party as she always wanted to see happy faces in the college.

We went to one of the tent houses and the owner was surprised to see me as I had worked for an ad film. He clicked selfies with me.

"Sir how can I help you?"

“Actually we have planned a farewell party in the college and I want some decorations and other stuff"

"Sure sir, I would definitely love to do it"

"What's the cost we have to pay? “I asked him.

The total cost will be 25000 including lights, decoration, and kinds of stuff. But sir, I will give you a 50% discount as you are my first celebrity customer.

My friends and I were very happy and I got treated like a VIP. Our problem was solved. We were left with 14,000 and that was enough for the snacks and cold drinks. We instructed girls to wear western dress and boys too. I was a kind of manager of the event. I wasn't doing anything physically but everything was under my supervision. And I was reporting everything to Nisha mam. We are excited because it was our first organized event in the college and we really worked hard for it.

Hardik and Manushi danced together and we saw them gracing the dance floor. It was really pleasant to see them dancing.

"Will you dance with me Souvik?" asked Preeti.

I was surprised and happy to hear that question.

"Yes Preeti, I would love to dance with you," I replied.

The party ended at 9:30 pm and we wrapped up everything by 10 pm.

The next day, I got a letter.

"Dear Souvik

Hope you are doing great. We are happy to announce that we are making a song album in which Avneet Kaur would be our leadership role and we are searching for another male lead role.

Our music director Mika Singh and we discussed casting you.

If you are willing to do so then please email us at maddockproduction@gmail.com or feel free to contact us at 9848******.

Address: West Mumbai, Film city

Maddock production house."

I was so happy and my happiness was out of control after reading the letter. I ran and gave this good news to my friends. They were happy too except for Preeti.

"Why are you making such ripen face?" I asked Preeti

"Now you will be famous and you will not get time to spend with me and you will enjoy with the heroines" she replied

"Are you out of mind, I'll always be with you... till my last breath"

We really enjoyed that day and I called up the given number and I was requested to give a final audition in the month of December.

2nd December 2028: It was a bright chilly morning and was off to give my audition. Besides audition, I was moreover excited to meet Avneet Kaur she was just awesome and of course my childhood crush. He was elder than me but not so much. I went to the audition room and some people came to click photos with me as I worked in the pressure cooker ad.

"Please excuse him" A lady uttered.

She was assisted as my personal assistant. She was glamorous enough to be my assistant. I went to submit my profiles and gave a final audition. I gave my hundred percent and it did wonders. I was paid with a huge amount. It was a cheque of 5 lakhs. I was too happy to get that check in my hand. After I completed my audition, I was dropped at the office of Mika Singh, and that too in a BMW car.

I was getting good treatment over there. "May I come in" I took the permission.

"Yes ...Yes please" Mika Singh permitted. It was a cheering moment as Avneet was too with Mika Singh. We discussed our album. At last, we clicked selfies and photos and I was curious to share them in my Instagram profile.

I got a verification badge on my Instagram and Facebook profile.

I got a lot of advantages and gained a lot of popularity. Avneet too shared the pictures on her profile and I almost got 150k followers on Instagram.

We did many romantic scenes which I think Preeti didn't like.

The album was finally telecasted on YouTube and on television. My mother was happy seeing her son on television once again but my father was a bit despondent with my choice. He called me and told "Son, I just want you to, first, concentrate on completing your studies then you can carry on your acting career' . I did what my father said and I also credited the amount of 5 lacs to his bank account and requested him to donate some amount in the orphanage and some to the NGOs.

I wanted to give a car to my parents and I did that too. After a couple of weeks, I was gifted a Mahindra car which was almost around 18 lacs. We decided to pay the money in installments. My mother was proud of my success and my father too but the difference was that my father didn't want me to see that. After my graduation, we planned a trip to Kolkata. Manushi's maternal aunt used to live in Kolkata in a remote village that was half an hour away from the main city. The place was too green with lots of trees, bushes, and shrubs.

Every family had their personal ponds. Manushi's aunt Miss Payal used to live in a Villa and she also allowed us to spend our vacation there happily.

Near the villa, there was an unfinished building.

People said that it's haunted and that's why no one could ever finish the construction. We were just forbidden to enter that area. But we were those typical stubborn children, when we heard the word 'forbidden', we just knew what our next mission was.

“Please don't go there, it may be dangerous" Manushi warned us.

“Oh! Common there's nothing such as ghost and aatma." I told.

One such afternoon, when everybody was asleep, after having our lunch Hardik, Anubhav, and I stealthily escape from the house and went for playing to that building. We also invited Preeti, Aditi, and Manushi but they denied it. It was supposed to be a two-story building but it was an incomplete one so only a few stairs were built. We were having fun until we heard a loud noise. We were scared and we knew that it was now the time to run away. But as soon as we tried to run away Anubhav tripped over some rocks and fell down. The situation was turning worse. We both tried to pick him but he was becoming heavy with each passing minute. We chanted religious mantras that we had been taught and Anubhav became normal. We wasted no more time and ran away. We didn't tell about the incident but we were scared like hell. Since it's was a village, people tend to sleep early and wake up early. The place becomes totally dark after sunset. After feeding our dinner we were sent upstairs to sleep. We insisted to keep our lights switched on but Ms. Payal didn't listen and turned them off but the light of the balcony was switched on. Ms. Payal went downstairs. We three scared triplets were trying our best to sleep but all in vain. Then I saw someone standing outside on the balcony. I kept staring at that thing for more than five minutes and signaled Hardik and Anubhav to look at that. We saw someone standing there, facing us. We realized that it was a female as we saw long hair waving as the wind was blowing outside. We were about to shout for help when we heard a voice saying "ssssshhh....Chitkar noy, nahole bache thakbi na"(don't shout else you won't be alive anymore)

We probably fainted. We remember nothing and thought to book a cheap hotel and leave that village. After a few days, we got to know that a woman was murdered in that building and since it is said to be haunted.

My whole trip when scary we visited the famous Museum, Victoria Memorial. Our visit to Kolkata was a memorable one. Our happy Days went very soon and was time for us to settle our careers.

A HAPPY ENDING

Our life took a sudden change, Preeti and I were set apart from each other. The distance was too long. She went to Italy for her further studies and I settled in western Madhya Pradesh. My dream of becoming an actor was set aside as my family didn't support me.

I was a bit attracted to the profession of an IAS officer.

I did coaching for better understanding but I also continued with my content writing job and I also got many opportunities to narrate my story to the film directors. But Preeti was still in my heart. I used to chat with her in social networking platforms. Days passed by and we were getting busy day by day. My father gifted me a car as my serials were doing super well. It was my first time driving up a steep incline. The problem was not so much with driving up but it was that I was stuck behind a car that had abruptly stopped. Damn! I cursed as I applied the brakes.

The car in front of me had just begun to move when it halted again a few feet ahead. I tried to do the same. But I failed miserably. You see, the second I released the brake to press the accelerator, my car began rolling backward. Reflexively, I hit my right foot back onto the brake paddle. The vehicle immediately came to rest. Phew!

I realized this was going to be tricky. You need to be quick with this whole shifting from the brake to the accelerator thing-I told myself. I took a deep breath and went for it again.

The second attempt was unlike the first. The first had been better.

I shifted from brake to accelerator effortlessly, but I fumbled while releasing the clutch at the same time. This juggling was challenging enough for me on level ground, this time the race was also against gravity! It was quite a circus!

It required understanding, experience, and a cool head, none of which I possessed at that moment. My car continued to roll back. I panicked and slammed hard on the accelerator. The engine roared. I hated being in that situation and I came out of my car and kicked it hard. The car rolled down and I shouted *'Ruko, Ruko'*.

The card just hit the flower shop.

'Oh no!' I shouted.

'You bloody driver!!' The flower shop owner yelled at me.

'I am really sorry for this' I apologized.

"Ghanta sorry, Paisa nikalo" he angrily insulted me on the road filled with numerous people. I turned towards my pocket and gave 5000 rupees.

'Is it enough?' I questioned him in an innocent tone.

'Hmmm.....you please leave'. He politely taunted me.

I was like 'Mother Earth, Please swallow me'.

Months passed by and I started missing Preeti a lot but I was helpless. I started preparing for my UPSC exams but every time, I sat to study, her face always used to come in front of me. I was not able to concentrate and contacted some social influencers. Their advice was helpful and I followed them too.

I studied more than 12 hours a day and got tired and exhausted as I never did this earlier. I often slept hungry.

My mom called me every day to ask about my health and I never left her disappointing by saying that I slept without having food. But, she was my mom and she caught me in a minute.

"Don't lie to me, I very well know, you are not keeping well. If this happens, next time, then I will come there"

My father was whispering "if you go there, Mera aur Papa ka kya hoga?".

"Sorry, I will keep myself healthy and no need to worry mama"

23rd Feb 2029: I was ready to give my examination. The first round was prelims which I completed and succeeded in it successfully.

4th April 2029: It was time to apply for the mains and I found it bit difficult. I waited for the result and I was depressed knowing that I was not able to complete this round. Again I started preparing for my exams.

One night, I missed Preeti a lot and requested her to make a video call. I was again happy after a long time, seeing Preeti.

She literally cried as she was also missing me. She introduced me to her new friend 'Alex', he was also handsome but not more than me. I felt jealous but still I controlled. I was least interested to talk to him. His English ruined me. After talking to Preeti, I felt too relaxed. The next morning was beautiful, at least to me, it was. Sunlight streamed through the sheer curtains of our apartment and I could hear birds chirping from a distance. As usual, a UPSC aspirant's day started boring.

I sat down on my chair, opened the books and started reading. It was 9 a.m., when I started studying and time passed to 6:00 p.m....as we know time flies

I went out to chill myself and meanwhile I saw that in a deserted road, there was a girl, shouting for help.

I went close to her and saw that she was Shivani, who lived near my apartment.

No, I didn't go to fight with those hooligans.

There were almost four boys who were trying to molest Shivani. I was muddled in the situation and no idea flashed me at that moment. There was a small shop which was closed. I went to hide behind the shop and called the police but till then I was supposed to save her.

I threw a big stone towards them. One of the hooligans fell down and was hurt severely.

The other two started searching and shouting 'who is throwing stones? Come in front'

One of the hooligans slapped Shivani and told: "I know somebody from your side is doing this".

Shivani was crying for help. The man again slapped. I ran towards the boy with a stone in aggression and bagged him down and told Shivani to run away. They all gathered together and started hitting me, till then I gave a punch in one of the man's private part. He fell down with pain. I did the same with everyone and then I started hitting them and I was the hero of the story. For the time being, the police arrived and praised me. After saving Shivani a hero kind of feeling aroused in me.

The police dragged them in their van. She came running and hugged me and declared me as her brother. We went to the society and there, Shivani's family came to my house with the bouquet to thank me. Shivani's father was a newspaper editor and published about me in his newspaper all over India. Shivani came with a rakhi to me to tie on my wrist and I was left with no gift.

The ruffians hurt me too. There were scratches and I was injured. I took a rest that whole day.

12 April 2029: Preeti completed her higher studies and she was in search of a job. She advised me to clear my UPSC exams as soon as possible and wished me all the best. Months passed by and the day came for the exam. I got

the post of an IPS officer but I preferred diversity which I found better in an IAS officer.

While preparing for my UPSC exams, I got to know that confidence and commitment is needed much than hard work.

I postponed my IPS post for one year and prepared for an IAS officer again. The third time, I was nervous but somehow I gave my prelims, mains, and mock interview.

3rd August 2031: I was waiting for the result to get declared at 10:00 a.m. Finally, I entered my roll number and closed my eyes. I was too delighted to see that I got the posting of an IAS officer in the district of East singhbhum (a district in Jharkhand).

I informed this good news to my parents and Preeti. That happiness was just priceless.

I got busy with my duty and work. I got two personal bodyguards and uncountable benefits.

My parents preferred to stay in their own house which was too in East singhbhum. I was invited to the Raj Bhavan and the governor of Jharkhand congratulated me. It was a proud moment for me to handle the chair of an IAS officer. I was tied with numerous responsibilities. The next day I went to take the oath and I was nervous to meet the chief minister.

31 August 2031: That day India bagged the cricket World Cup. Virat's magnificent innings had led India to the victory. I am a die-hard fan of Virat and I guess somewhere the entire nation is a fan of him. The entire

nation was celebrating the victory. Cricket is a religion in India and winning is a festival. It had been a year since I spoke to Preeti.

Preeti got a job in the world Yes Bank. She was now ready to travel India back. I was planning to surprise Preeti by reaching Italy suddenly. I was in the flight. I reached Italy and went to Preeti's residence. I saw drops of blood giving me the way towards her apartment.

Her apartment was in a Hotel Florida and when I opened the door, I saw Preeti dead.

She was shot. Instantly someone clapped and my dream was left incomplete. I was sweating and immediately called Preeti but her phone was unreachable. I was strained and anxious. The moment, the flight landed, I ran to Preeti. I knocked on the door and I was happy to see her in a good condition.

I gave her a hug and kissed her on her forehead. A glance of her made my heart beat faster. She was astonished and surprised to see me and was happy too.

"Welcome DC Sahab" she giggled and welcomed me.

I haven't seen more beautiful girl than Preeti but she had something which made her look very attractive. Whenever she was around, the world seemed to be like a movie, slow motion walk, music in the background, and of course the breeze.

Preeti and I went for a candlelight dinner. We spoke for hours, we literally shared everything and we ordered some special dish of Italy. It was Risotto, Bagna cauda and pizza.

The next day, we left for India, Jamshedpur.

We thought to talk to our parents about our marriage. 'If my parents approve you, I will marry you' she said.

She was ready to marry me. I want to talk to my parents. They agreed to our marriage but with some hesitation and also they rejected several times.

"We are ok with Preeti being our Bahu. If Souvik wants to marry her, she has our blessings." My father told. Preeti's mother liked me since school days but never knew that I like her daughter.

I went to Preeti's house with my parents with my bodyguards too.

I was respected a lot in Preeti's house I was the IAS officer of the district. They requested 'Kundali'.

"Beta would you not demand any dowry (dahej)?" Preeti's father enquired.

"Bhaiya hamare pass bhagwan ka diya hua sab kuchh hai, hamari koi demands nahin hai" My mother told with a sweet smile.

It was a big step for both the families to do an inter caste marriage.

It took months to convince our parents but finally we were going to be life-partners and it was unbelievable...

We got engaged on 5th August 2032 and then officially went out for a few weeks, before we got married. Yes, there were a lot of relatives from Preeti's side and as well as mine, who didn't approve of this decision. But it didn't matter at all as Preeti and I was happy together along with our families.

Yes, I married my crush. The love of my life, Preeti.

Haardik, Manushi, Anubhav, and Aditi were too invited to attend my marriage reception.

Aditi was married too, with Kaushal and their love story was also a bit interesting. There were ACP's, DGP's and many high officials.

The chief minister and other ministers also attended our marriage ceremony. We planned for a honeymoon to Goa. The pressure was crushing. I wanted to spend my whole honeymoon romantic but Preeti was dumb in matters of romance.

We spent seven days, six months in Goa, and had a lot of fun.

Days passed by and we both were happy together.

Preeti got pregnant and we couldn't have become happier.

She soon left her job and started staying at home. I was happy and worried both at the same time. Happy because my family was about to complete and worried as I didn't want anything wrong to happen to my newly formed family.

In the last few years of my life, I have seen everything. I never thought that life would take such a serious turn but I was happy.

I married the girl who was my everything now. I woke up with terrible screaming. Preeti was yelling out of pain. I shouted and called out my staff but it was Sunday and nobody was available. I took out the car and was on the way to the nearest hospital. I was in a hurry and it was bit dark. We were passing through a highway and a truck driver was fully drunk and we met an accident.

Preeti was lying on the road and all covered in blood. She didn't move an inch. I was not able to stand, I too got severe hurts. I tried to crawl towards her but there was no response.

There were travellers who were just watching and didn't even tried to admit us to the nearby hospital. One of our district inspectors Mr. Prakash Singh admitted both of us to the hospital. Preeti's health was severe and she was in the ICU.

Doctors were not at all ready to attend to her as it was a police case but as soon as they saw me, they ran towards for a check-up.

Doctors said that Preeti is very serious and everything now depends on the almighty. However, I walked up to Preeti and said "You cannot do this to me! You promised to stay with me forever. Wake up Preeti, wake up. Don't do this to me."

I was crying literally, was speechless, and was literally numb. I had no clue what to do. The doctor entered and requested me to leave and at last, they came up with the final report. "It's very disappointing to say that, sir you have to choose only one of them, Preeti or your upcoming child. The doctor added.

I without any hesitation chose Preeti to live with me. As I thought that a child can take birth again but my love can't.

Preeti got hurt on her leg but she was safe. She cried a lot and said "Sorry Souvik, I was unable to save our child"

I patted her and took the situation lightly but the pain that she carried for 9 months was just a moment of salutation.

Preeti's family and my family were literally disappointed.

The doctor came up with another bad news that Preeti can't give birth to a child anymore due to some severe medical purpose.

It was hard for her to come out of such a great depression.

After a couple of months, we decided to adopt a child from the orphanage. We informed our parents and they were proud of our decision. As for now, we decided as adoption as a better option. We named our daughter 'Shruti'.

After a few months, we were invited to our school alumni function. We all friends gathered and I was given VIP treatment. Our memories were discussed and our love story made history. Hardik didn t marry Manushi as Manushi's family didn't accept Hardik.

It was a sad and disappointing moment for them but still, Hardik had the capability to cope with that moment. They both tackled the situation.

We enjoyed our alumni function. We did some enjoyment and also performed.

Preeti and I started living in the Villa which was provided by the government and now Preeti was the chief manager of ICICI Bank. We started up with an NGO. Life was almost set. "I love you Preeti, I love you ......and nobody can replace you. You are forever with me."

Glossary

PREETI

SOUVIK

ADITI

MANUSHI

SHWETA

HAARDIK

ANUBHAV

List of Contributors

COVER PAGE: ROHIT KAR AND PRIYA CHOUDHRY

BOOK TITLE: K.DIXITA

NIHARIKA TIWARY

IF U LOVED THE BOOK THEN DM THE AUTHOR ON INSTAGRAM @its__real__soumyaranjan OR EMAIL AT @joinauthorsoumya@gmail.com

www.ingramcontent.com/pod-product-compliance
Lightning Source LLC
LaVergne TN
LVHW050415160726
843469LV00041B/1083

* 9 7 8 9 3 5 6 1 0 0 6 3 3 *